A CLAP OF THUNDER ROARED
at exactly the moment my grandmother came
into the world during a raging storm in 1883
on her parents' farm in Locke Center, Michigan.
She was the first of nine children. "And
look here," the midwife said, "she's born in a
Mermaid's Purse!" A birth membrane to some,
a miracle to others. "God's blessing and gifts
will fall upon this child like spring rain."

My grandmother's name became Estella,
for the bright star shining low in the night sky
after the storm passed by, but she was drawn to
storms, and storms to her, the rest of her life.
And the Mermaid's Purse? Well, now here's
the story.

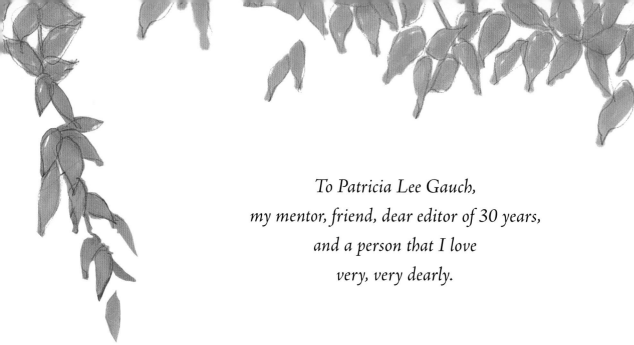

To Patricia Lee Gauch,
my mentor, friend, dear editor of 30 years,
and a person that I love
very, very dearly.

Patricia Lee Gauch, Editor

G. P. PUTNAM'S SONS
am imprint of Penguin Random House LLC
375 Hudson Street, New York, NY 10014

G. P. Putnam's Sons is a registered trademark of Penguin Random House LLC.

Library of Congress Cataloging-in-Publication Data is available upon request.
Manufactured in China by RR Donnelley Asia Printing Solutions Ltd.
ISBN 978-0-399-16692-1
1 3 5 7 9 10 8 6 4 2

Design by Siobhán Gallagher. Text set in 15-point Adobe Jenson Pro.
The illustrations are rendered in pencils and markers.

The Mermaid's Purse

Patricia Polacco

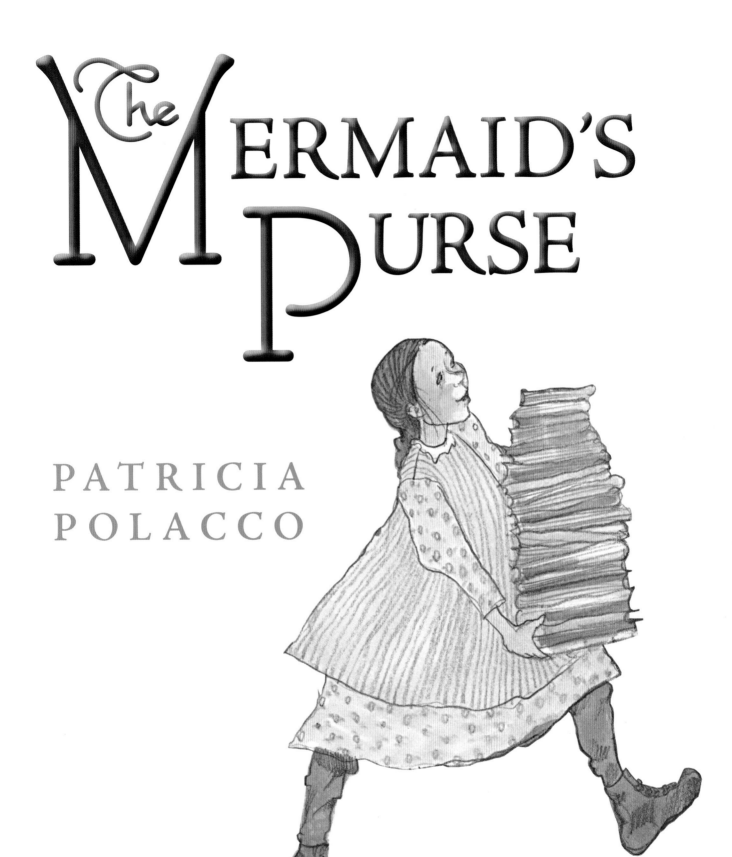

G. P. PUTNAM'S SONS

Blessings and gifts surely did come to little Estella, just as the midwife predicted. She walked at eight months and spoke in full at a year.

And every time a storm threatened, it was as if Estella knew it was coming long before the sky darkened. When the thunder exploded with window-rattling fury, she'd smile and stretch out her little hands and peer into the sky as if to receive a gift.

What Stella loved more than anything—from the time she was a baby—was being read to every night until she drifted off to sleep.

As soon as Stella could stretch her right arm over the top of her own head and grasp her left ear, she was sent off to school! She taught herself to read.

From that time on, it seemed she always had her nose in a book—churning butter, kneading bread, feeding the sheep and goats. When Stella needed to be alone, she'd steal away and read.

After a while Stella started collecting books. She bought them at church bazaars with money she made selling her apple butter. Or she'd trade a portrait she'd painted for a beautifully bound book!

Soon there were so many books, they took up the entire upper floor of the farmhouse. She loved every one.

"Stella," her father said to her one day, "looks like I'm going to have to build you your very own library for all these books!"

And sure enough, one day a whole crew of her father's friends showed up and built a dear little library for all her books.

One of them was young Fred Barber, a rosy-cheeked apprentice. Seemed like whenever she was watching them build the new library, young Fred was watching her.

"That lad is making moon eyes at you, Stellie," her pa teased. Finally the building was finished, and all of the men helped carry the books from the farmhouse into the new library with Stella carrying her share, too.

"Why in tarnation does that fool girl want all of these here books," Pig Ears Lonsberry snorted. "Alls they do is take up room!"

Just as they carried the last bundle of books into the library, there was
a rumbling in the distance. Stella stood up and got that faraway look in
her eyes and walked to the door. Menacing clouds were moving swiftly down
the holler.

She stretched out her arms and her hands filled with cool rain, christening
the library. She smiled. "I'm calling this building the Mermaid's Purse. I was
born in one, and it blessed my life, just like these books do."

That night at the dinner table, Stella told her father how some of the men didn't seem to care a whit about books. "They scoffed at them— and me, Pa."

"Stella, my guess is that they haven't ever read a book," her father said matter-of-factly.

"Well then, Pa, tomorrow I'm going to take books around to all of the farmers. See if I can at least get folks to open one!"

The very next day she loaded up her goat cart and took her books from farm to farm. At each stop she was welcomed—"Hello, Miss Stella. Nice to see you, Miss Stella." Children came over to the library afternoons to hear Stella read stories right off, but none of the farmers seemed eager to actually take a book.

Then one hot and sticky afternoon, Eldon Dunkle's pa came skidding into the farmyard in his wagon. "There's something powerful wrong with my sheep, Frank!" he bellowed at Stella's pa. "Come quick!"

Stella ran to the little library and grabbed two books, then jumped in the back of Pa's buckboard and raced to the Dunkle farm with him.

When she and her pa got there, sheep could be seen lying on their sides all over the pasture, bloated and motionless. Pa raised cattle, not sheep, so he wasn't sure what to do! Stella was reading a very thick book, furiously.

"Pa . . . Mr. Dunkle . . . I think I know," she called out as she jumped from the buckboard. "It's been unseasonably hot, right? The timothy sprouted sooner than it should've, and, it says here, early timothy can cause sheep to build gas in their bellies. If you don't remedy it, the sheep could die."

"Remedy it?" bellowed Dunkle. "How?"

"Look here at this page. It says you have to pierce the sheep's hide, right behind the rib cage, but in front of the haunches. That will let the air out!"

With that, Mr. Dunkle, Stella's pa and other farmers set about puncturing the bloated sheep's bellies. As they did, there was a rush of air and the sheep brayed, and then jumped to their feet, none the worse for wear.

Dunkle took the book in his hands and waved it. "This book saved my sheep!" he bleated. "I guess, Miss Stella, these books matter more than I ever did think!"

One day, Stella was riding through Aunt Eliza's woods. When she came upon the swimming hole, she saw some boys she knew.

"Come on in, Stellie," someone called out to her.

It was Moon Eyes Fred! Other boys teased him about liking her.

Stella jumped down from her horse, kicked off her shoes, tucked her skirt into her belt, and dove in. Of course she could swim better than any of them, even with that skirt tucked into her belt.

She swam to a large rock in the center of the pond.
She had no more than scrambled up on it when she
heard a low rumbling off in the distance. The
sky was darkening and the clouds glowed
with shards of lightning.

"Get out of the water!" she
warned the boys.

All scrambled out but one. Moon Eyes Fred.

"Fred!" she shouted. "Thunderstorms are something I know about. That lightning is closer than you think."

No sooner had she said those words than there was a bright flash of light and Fred disappeared beneath the surface of the water. Stella jumped in and pulled him to shore. She rolled him on his back, put her mouth over his and pushed small bursts of air into him.

"Stellie, what crazy thing you doing?" one of the boys shouted.

"I read about this in a book. It's what they do in England to revive drowning victims." Stella panted between puffs.

The skies opened up just above them and raindrops as big as bumblebees pelted their backs as they knelt around Fred. Suddenly Fred's eyes fluttered and he started coughing up pond water! He was okay.

From then on Fred Barber was almost never out of Stella's sight.

Every week, Stella faithfully made her rounds to the farms with her goat cart full of books. Now just about everyone took a book or two. They particularly liked a good story. But not Pig Ears Lonsberry. He refused to even look at a book.

One winter day, she pulled her sleigh into Pig Ears Lonsberry's farm. "Mr. Lonsberry!" she sang out. "I have a book right here in my hand that you are going to love!" He loved roses, and the book was all about roses.

Pig Ears didn't look up. "You're interrupting me, girl," he grumbled.

There was a man standing behind him with a fistful of papers. "Pig Ears," he said, "you're going to have to read these documents and sign them, or you're gonna lose your water rights." He climbed into his buggy. "You don't have much time!"

Stella watched Pig Ears try to understand the papers clutched in his hand. Why, they were upside down! Pig Ears Lonsberry couldn't read!

"Mr. Lonsberry, I can teach you to read," Stella whispered as she touched his hand. "Come to the library on an afternoon, after the children leave."

Pig Ears raised his brow. Not sure at all.

Just then, the sky caught Stella's attention. "A blizzard is coming!"

"Now, how would you know that. It's as clear as a bell out," Pig Ears countered.

But that afternoon the snow fell, and a storm blew through the county, just as she'd said.

He'd take a chance on Stella after all. In a few months Pig Ears Lonsberry could read. Fact is, he borrowed more books than all of the other farmers and farmers' wives combined!

Now everyone in the county knew and loved Stella and the Mermaid's Purse and its wonderful books.

Then one sultry summer afternoon, Stella and Fred were sitting on the front porch swing when suddenly Stella stood up. A look of alarm came over her face. She gazed toward the horizon in the southwest.

"Something is coming, Fred. You'd better head for home."

A far off look came over her face and Fred knew it was useless

to convince her otherwise. When it came to storms, she was always right.

After he left, Stella stood, staring at the sky. Sure enough, a darkness started appearing far, far away, but moving at a great speed toward them.

"Quick!" Stella warned her eight brothers and sisters. "Into the storm cellar!"

Almost instantly, the very air outside turned a greenish yellow.
It was still. Clouds, smoky black and churning, circled overhead, and
suddenly all of the doors in the house slammed shut. Stella's father
grabbed her by the arm and pulled her and her mother
into the storm cellar, too.

A screaming wind began to rage overhead, then glass crashed
and heavy things were hurled at the ground.

"It's a twister!" Stella's father called out as he put his arms
around all of them.

It seemed to last forever, but probably lasted only minutes. Finally Pa
pushed open the storm door. When the family came out, they were stunned.

All of the tall luxurious green trees had been scoured bare. The house had
only one wall standing, and heaps of broken boards were thrown all over the
yard. Two of the beautiful spreading oaks were ripped from the ground.

And the Mermaid's Purse? Gone. Not a shelf, not a floorboard. Not a book.

The whole family went to stay at Aunt Mabel and Uncle Wayland's just down the hollow—the twister hadn't touched their house. "I saw this funnel coming for yours. It looked like it was walking!" Aunt Mabel said.

Stella came down with a strange malady after that day. "The shock of losing all of her books must have been too much for her," her mother said if anyone inquired. Stella just sat in the three-corner window looking at the garden and flowers with a powerful sadness, not saying anything. Not a word. She just seemed to be somewhere else.

Fred Barber never left her side.

As fall came to Locke Center, burning leaves sent up gray sweet-smelling smoke. Bright orange pumpkins were plumping the fields. The sound of hammering of new houses sounded all across the hill. But Stella just couldn't bear to look at the hill. Not where the Purse had been.

Then one day Stella's pa loaded the whole family into the buckboard. "There's something I want you all to see," their father said.

There, near where the old house had been, stood a beautiful new house. Fred took Stella's hand and led her to the new porch. "And look, Stella, over there. We've rebuilt the Mermaid's Purse." Stella turned her head away. "But the books," she whispered. "My beautiful books."

That was when her youngest sister, Ivah, called out, "Look, Stella . . . a parade . . . just for you!" Stella turned slowly and looked down the road. There, as far she could see, were buckboards, surreys and wagons filled with books. All of them coming up the hill.

As the first wagon arrived, Pig Ears Lonsberry climbed down. "Miss Stellie," he began. "All of us've been finding your books, all over the countryside—been gathering 'em, drying 'em on our clotheslines, a little worse for wear from all that water, but many, good as new."

One by one the wagons pulled into the yard. Farm folks trundled out with baskets or armloads of books. Hoot Haggerty, Kutch McCafferty, Eldie Dunkle, Hefrie Petit, Lyn Crossman and Louis Liverance to name a few. Her precious books were finding their way back to her.

"We love you, Stellie," someone shouted. "You brought the world to us through your books, so we brought them back to you and the Mermaid's Purse."

"Yes." She was looking at the new library now with all its new books. "You certainly did."

WORDS FROM PATRICIA POLACCO FOR HER READERS

After that, my grandmother recovered fully and opened her Mermaid's Purse again, and she kept it open even after she completed teachers' training and became a teacher and librarian right there in Locke Center. She married her darling Fred Barber, Moon Eyes, and they remained together for almost sixty years. Eventually my grandmother left Locke Center and taught in Williamston, a town nearby. She donated her amazing library to the public library of Williamston, where books from it still remain today.

My grandmother's wedding to
"Moon-eyes Fred" in 1901

Estella Barber
c. 1951

My grandmother and some of the
children she taught and read to
in front of The Mermaid's Purse
c. 1925